When We're Up Against It

(Real Life Examples)

Sharon Slaton Howell

Black Wolf Press
2017

Printed in the USA

Published by:
  Black Wolf Press
  1800 Grand Avenue
  Knoxville, Tennessee 37916

Printed and bound in the United States of America.

6th Printing

Library of Congress Control Number: 2015910867

Table of Contents

Six Year Old Girl

When someone's life has been as full of God's help in challenging conditions as mine has been, it doesn't seem right to keep quiet about it. So I won't.

My first recollection of this was when we lived in Dallas, Texas. I had just started grade school a little while before, and was playing in a friend's yard behind our house. She had a swing set, and this particular day, I happened to slide down one of the poles onto an unsealed, razor-sharp, peanut can.

An account of this appeared recently in The New York Times at the invitation of one of the Editors. They were doing an article on children and their health.

The cut went almost through the top of my foot. My father was at home, and the father of my friend yelled at him to come out of the house. He lifted me over the fence to my father, who carried me to a bedroom.

My mother, who had begun studying Christian Science a little before this, and had had healings

herself, wanted to call a Christian Science practitioner to pray for me. My dear father was not of this religion, not really religious at all, and with not much faith in doctors over all. But he consented to my having prayerful help. The woman my mother phoned said she'd begin praying for me at once. The only thing done was my foot was washed off and clean cloths wrapped around it. Very soon, I was told, the bleeding completely stopped. The best part of this to me was that I actually *felt* God's presence. I wasn't afraid at all. While it may be difficult for some readers to believe, I could put weight on this foot the very next day, and within three days I was back at school, walking and playing as before.

This wonderful proof of what prayer can do no doubt was the basis of a life-long reliance on divine help. Moreover, this healing made quite an impression on my father who later began relying on Christian Science himself when he lost his job and couldn't find work.

A Fall Day in New England

There I was one beautiful October day in New England, going from shop to shop on errands. Out of the blue, as I had just turned from an alleyway between two stores, Bam! A boy on a bicycle who was racing another boy (on the sidewalk, no less) crashed into me. This not only knocked me to the ground, but also injured one of my hands in the process. It felt like a bone was broken. People gathered around to help, and though I felt shaken, I didn't want to try getting up just then. "I'll be all right", I assured them. After leaning against a wall, for perhaps twenty minutes or so, I was able to get to the parking lot nearby, then carefully drive myself home.

The pain was intense. But I knew from years of experience that God is always present to heal us. I felt confident relying totally on this spiritual power rather than seeking medical treatment. That first night was rough. But I prayed fervently to realize my selfhood as God's spiritual image and likeness. I reminded myself that man as made by God--my true and *only* identity--was spiritual, not material, and not subject to physical suffering. I was able to use my hand by the next evening. Regaining complete strength took a few

days more. But all considered, this was a very quick return to normality.

Even before I got up to walk to my car and go home that afternoon, I remembered a passage from *Science and Health with Key to the Scriptures* by Mary Baker Eddy that was especially helpful to me right then. It's where she writes: "When an accident happens, you think or exclaim, 'I am hurt!' Your thought is more powerful than your words, more powerful than the accident itself, to make the injury real." In the next paragraph she continues, "Now reverse the process. Declare that you are not hurt and understand the reason why, and you will find the ensuing good effects to be in exact proportion to your disbelief in physics, and your fidelity to divine metaphysics, confidence in God as All, which the Scriptures declare Him to be."

I appreciate the help this and similar statements of spiritual truths give in cases of bodily injury for many reasons, most of all, the instant availability of their healing power. Instead of waiting for EMTs to reach the scene or for a ride to a hospital or doctor's office to begin treatment, we can begin getting help the very instant a need arises. As the Bible states: "Am I a God at hand, saith the Lord, and not a God

afar off?…Do not I fill heaven and earth? saith the Lord" While the five physical senses report that we're not always in God's presence, the fact remains that we cannot find ourselves beyond His help, cannot be in a place where God is not.

Because of the Bible's assurances that God, divine Love, is an ever-present, unfailing help in trouble, we can turn in complete confidence to Him. No matter what situation we may find ourselves in, God's help is always right there, even--or more accurately, *especially*--when the need is urgent.

Christ Jesus taught us the inseparability of man from God. We're able to see the effects of this truth as we live in harmony with the divine will. As Jesus said, "He that sent me is with me: the Father hath not left me alone; for I do always those things that please him."

Knowing that man is God's child, wholly spiritual and safe in the care of his creator, regardless of appearances, the Master was able to heal. And Jesus' works bring to light the fact that man can't fall from his original spiritual state of perfection and freedom as the offspring of God. Through understanding that our real being is spiritual, and

making a sincere effort to be obedient to God in our lives, each one of us can know the comforting assurance of divine Love's care, whatever the challenge may be.

Man's true selfhood, as the outcome of Spirit, God, is spiritual, not material. Thus that man--our real identity--is not at the mercy of accident, injury, or disease. The divine fact is that you and I are God's child, and we can never, for an instant, be deprived of our Father's loving care. We're never really out of our God-provided place of spiritual security. We can't be apart from our divine source, God. As God's man, we are always preserved by His unerring laws of order, safety, and exemption from harm. Such divine facts give us the authority and confidence we need to heal injury and pain.

Another quick recuperation from an injury happened a few years ago. I was hiking through a wooded area some streets over from us, and jumped over a fence when nearly home. The fence wasn't so high actually, it's just that I landed crooked. The pain in my ankle was severe. I managed to hobble into the house, and as my husband was standing there in the kitchen, I asked him to help me prayerfully with this problem. The rest of that afternoon and evening was

very difficult, especially needing to go up and down stairs. When I got in bed that night, even the slightest touch of my ankle against the sheet was a challenge. Not much sleep that night for sure.

But to my relief, when I got out of bed the next morning, I could place a little pressure on this foot. This encouraged me to keep praying. Improvement continued all that day, and by evening I found I could attend a homeowner's meeting around the next cul-de-sac. I did have to go down some stairs to their basement for the meeting, which I had to take slowly. And most interesting, our host was in a chair with one foot propped up on another chair. He told us he had badly injured his ankle playing basketball. And this is the part that stood out to me: the doctor said he'd be off that leg for about six weeks. And there I was just about fully recovered. What a contrast this is with my situation, I couldn't help thinking.

Feeling almost one hundred percent back to easy mobililty, I decided to do some errands in the next town. I was shuffling along a street there in Needham, Massachusetts, having just left their lovely library, when something happened I've never forgotten. A spiritual insight stopped me cold on the sidewalk. With crystal clarity, I saw that the injury and

pain were not part of me, had *never* been part of me. "Why, I don't have to creep along with this difficulty. There's no need for gradual improvement. This never happened to me as God's reflection!"

Instantly, I felt something being adjusted physically. The remaining discomfort disappeared. While it's hard to put into words, I knew and felt that I was completely healed, right then and there. I walked on freely and normally. This experience showed me the mental nature of recuperation.

Mrs. Eddy writes in *Unity of Good*, "Jesus required neither cycles of time nor thought in order to mature fitness for perfection and its possibilities." Time does not actually enter into spiritual healing. Why is this? Because what appears to be a physical problem is, in reality, wholly mental. It is but a phase of mortal belief, objectified. As it becomes clear that we're not dealing with a real condition that needs to be changed but only with an erroneous mental state, a misconception of man's true spiritual identity, we stop being afraid of or impressed with debility. What appears real to erring human belief is not a reality to man in God's likeness. It has never been real at all. Our need, therefore, is always for a change of consciousness from a material to a spiritual basis, to

the recognition that God is perfect and that we are His perfect, spiritual reflection--now and forever. This enlightened mental state is then objectified in our experience as healing, as normality and freedom.

As it was for me in both the experiences I've shared.

Encounter in Our Woods

And what I encountered was a patch of poison ivy. We had just moved from Boston, Massachusetts to our new home in Tennessee. It was at the edge of a lovely forest (well, woods actually, but full of huge trees and lush undergrowth.) Being a tree lover I couldn't wait to explore. In doing so, I happened to wander into a lot of poison ivy. I was healed of this finally, but it wasn't much fun working out of it prayerfully. This went on much too long. The itching on my arms and legs was maddening, especially at night. And during this time, our realtor who had helped us with finding our new house and the move, invited my husband and me out to a nice restaurant for dinner one evening. I wasn't able to completely cover my arms, which she noticed as we were eating. Alarmed was one word to describe her reaction. I assured her something was being done to alleviate the condition, though I didn't give her the details of how it was being handled. I don't think she was particularly into religion, so further explanation wouldn't have meant much to her I decided.

Then last spring everyone in East Tennessee was talking about how prolific poison ivy was. People were being warned to steer clear of it. I realized the

importance of not opening thought up to suffering this time around and began applying some of the truths I knew from my study of Christian Science as a preventive measure. I prayed from the standpoint of man's exemption from disease due to his eternal unity with God. I realized the reassuring fact that as a divine reflection of God, we enjoy uninterrupted protection from the human mind's fears and false beliefs and the attendant distress.

It dawned on me when the neighbor I mentioned earlier was telling me about how careful she had been while gardening to wear long sleeves, gloves, long pants, and had still gotten poison ivy, why I've gone all summer, been in our woods countless times with our dogs, even been unexpectedly dragged through thickets with the feared plant when the chase was on for a cat or rabbit or squirrel and not been affected at all.

And speaking of "thickets", our high-spirited puppy once slipped his harness and took off one afternoon. For nearly an hour, I chased Dylan through densely-wooded areas in our neighborhood, up and down hills, in shorts, without a trace of the dreaded plant showing up on me. I have learned through the years that an understanding of God's laws not only cures disease; it prevents it as well.

Texas Mother:
Dramatically Healed

Up until the time I was about four years old, mother was a devoted Methodist, teaching Sunday School and happy with her church work. But there was a serious physical problem that made her life hellish at times. She had some inner ear disturbance and pain she had suffered since her teenage years. Different kind doctors had tried to relieve her, but to no avail. As one can imagine, with me and my little brother to care for, plus everything else a mother and wife has to do to keep the family going, life was trying for her. Daddy was there, working and providing for his family as best he could, which was a help.

Then one day a neighbor who knew of her problem came to visit. She mentioned that there was a book my mother might be interested in reading. It was *Science and Health* referred to earlier in this book. The woman told her she herself and others she knew had been healed through reading and pondering some of the things about God and man in it.

Mother knew nothing of this religion. What it taught was new to her. But she was desperate to

get some relief from the suffering, so she told the neighbor she'd at least look through the book.

Well, she was only part way through this book when she was freed---dramatically, completely, permanently from the physical condition. Her joy knew no bounds. She could hardly contain herself. Although highly dependent on pills of all kinds, she cleaned out the medicine cabinet and thereafter relied solely on God for health and well-being. She went wholeheartedly into the study of Christian Science, enrolled my brother and me in the Sunday School, and never looked back. Many were the later proofs of God's power she experienced in her very long life of practicing this religion.

Kansas School Teacher:
Only Months to Live

This young woman was happily teaching school in a small town in Kansas when she contracted tuberculosis. At first, her father who was a doctor, tried to treat her successfully. But he wasn't able to cure her, so she was taken to a nearby sanatorium for rest and hopefully a cure.

However, it wasn't long before the verdict came in: they gave her at most six more months to live. It was at this critical point in her life that something quite unexpected happened. One day a lady in the town who knew of her situation came to visit. She happened to be a Christian Scientist, and she told my friend of the many cures being brought about by the truths in *Science and Health*. My friend said at once, "Oh, give me the book that can do that for me!" A copy of this book was brought to her which she began reading, night and day. And the wonderful thing about this, she walked out of that facility completely and permanently free of the TB.

Not only this, she was on fire to help others gain the freedom and good health she had gained.

She spent the next six decades in the public practice of her new religion, taking thousands of cases needing help. Her dedicated work in Tulsa, Oklahoma reached way beyond that city and state, and impacted the lives of people all over the world who called on her for help.

   In my own case, many were the times I phoned this woman or went to see her for a way out of this or that problem. I always came away restored. Healed when healing of a physical difficulty was needed. And sometimes the need was urgent.

Writer From British Columbia: Eyesight Restored

This young man had just started work in an accounting firm in British Columbia when he began to have a challenge with his eyes. This was understandably alarming to him given the detailed work he was expected to do. Things did not improve over the months, and finally he had to leave his office work completely.

He tried different approaches to overcome his failing eyesight, even taking a trip to England to consult with a specialist there. This did not arrest the decline in his seeing. Month after month he sat in an almost completely darkened room so painful was the light for him.

It was then that his life changed. Someone mentioned a book to him that had helped many others with various health problems. It was *Science and Health*. Desperate for anything that would help, he got a copy of the book. Reading was of course very difficult, slow work. But Samuel Greenwood continued, receiving a glimmer of hope that he could overcome his problem. Already a very religious

Christian man, he was learning new things about God's laws he had never known before. That His laws supersede human beliefs, and that a radical change in thought from material beliefs and fears to a spiritual understanding of divine truths would bring healing, inspired him to keep on with his reading and praying.

His sight began coming back, and was completely restored. One can just imagine the freedom and joy this man felt! He felt the rest of his life must be given to what had set him free that others might be helped as he had been. At once he entered the public practice of Christian Science as a practitioner so that he might devote all his time to helping others in need. A church was started there in Victoria, B.C. He later became a teacher of Christian Science, holding annual classes to instruct others in this work.

This highly intelligent, I would have to say gifted, Christian thinker and writer had investigated all world religious thought he wrote, and had not found anything that matched Christian Science in being able to make plain to the reader the Master's healing method. Thus his lifelong devotion to his new-found religion.

Speaking for myself, the writings on meta-physical subjects which poured out of this man's pen are among the most inspiring I have ever read. Both my husband and I have all his addresses and owe much to Greenwood's crystal clear, uncompromising presentation of divine truths. The grasp he had of the English language, his ability to express ideas in a fresh and compelling way, the love he had for Jesus which was at the core of all he lived and taught and wrote about have led me to heaven's door. To think of what his discovering Christian Science for himself has done for many thousands all over the world.

I'll mention two things this man pointed out that have stayed with me: first, to quote his words: "It is a fatal mistake to relegate Jesus to a secondary place, in the divine plan of human salvation." How often I think of this when confronting those who in some strange way almost consider Jesus of not having that much importance in their lives, who do not take seriously Jesus' words nor strive to live by them. In short, who are putting everything else in life in first place instead of the Master's teachings. This is distressing to me, and so many times I've done my best to enlighten individuals on this vital issue.

And secondly, that lack of Christly love being expressed to others and felt for ourselves is the cause

of so much bodily suffering. He went further. He said that in decades of people calling on him for healing, in every instance, it was that there was insufficient divine love flowing through thought. They had lost the connection with God, as it were. If indeed it had ever been there at all.

We did not have the privilege of knowing Samuel Greenwood personally. But we do have so much of what he wrote, which continue to lift us up spiritually.

Tennessee Housekeeper: Self-Confidence Gained

Cyndi came to do some housework for us once a week. And one day she saw me at my desk reading something. Curious, she asked about the book. I told her it was *Science and Health with Key to the Scriptures*. She knew nothing about it, or the religion my husband and I were involved with, so I told her a little of what it taught and of our experiences in practicing it.

She asked if she could borrow the book. I had an extra copy, so gladly gave it to her. Over the next few weeks, she would say, I'm reading a little each day and finding some brand new thoughts in it.

Then one day she telephoned on a day that wasn't her regular time to clean. There was such excitement in her voice. She had come to page 89 in this book where Mrs. Eddy writes: "Mind is not necessarily dependent upon educational processes. It possesses of itself all beauty and poetry, and the power of expressing them." Cyndi couldn't stop reading and thinking about these words, she told me. They had

opened up a whole new world to her.

Being someone of very little formal schooling, she had felt inferior all her life. She had yearned to express herself better, wanted to be more active in her Baptist church, but never felt she was educated enough to try.

Just above the words that turned her thinking about herself right around, were these she read to me when she came over. Mrs. Eddy is talking about a person who says, "I am incapable of words that glow, for I am uneducated. If one believes that he cannot be an orator without study or a superinduced condition, the body responds to this belief, and the tongue grows mute which before was eloquent."

Cyndi's life was different from this time on. The change was noticeable to many people. Self-expression came much more confidently. This was one happy, dear, Christian girl.

Ohio Man:
Lifted Up From Invalidism

As a young man in Ohio, H. James Frost was seriously ill, too weak to get out of bed and take a ride in his parents' car. For many months, he was completely bedridden.

Then something wonderful happened, he told us, when we met him in Wellesley, Massachusetts where we all lived then. A neighbor mentioned a book to him he might find of interest. This was *Science and Health.* The book was obtained for him, and he started reading and thinking about what it pointed out. Jim (as his friends called him) said his healing was not quick. But little by little, his physical symptoms disappeared, and his strength came back. Complete freedom came eventually. He, too, decided to give the rest of his very long life to the public practice of Christian Science.

For years when I had an office for such work in an office building across from the Christian Science Church in Boston Jim's office was on the floor below. Many were the fruitful discussions we had, as well as his fine healing work when my husband and I needed

help. And as I say later in this book in more detail, the one that stands out is when I ran into a serious problem with my writing, and asked him "Whom can I take this problem to?" It was this very man who said what I'll never forget -- "Why not take it to God?" It was as though an angel had spoken and given me counsel which helped me countless times later.

I mentioned that Jim's strength came back to him. And so marked was his very energetic, full life that it inspired all who knew him. He later learned to fly, got a small plane, flew everywhere in Massachusetts, and to Ohio to visit relatives. He learned to ski. He studied carpentry from books in the Wellesley Public Library, adding an addition to their house. He hiked miles each day when he had the time away from his healing work. And one Sunday at the local church where we all attended, he was at the end of the parking lot when someone talking with us said, "Who is that college kid? Is he a new member?" Jim's posture, springy step, expression of agelessness was remarkable. I did not know his age, and was not interested in mortal years. It just didn't matter, as he seemed to transcend aging more than anyone I've ever known. His shining example of relying on God's power in everything he did will be remembered by those who knew and loved him.

Oklahoma Boy:
Surviving Iwo Jima

It was such a privilege to know this former Marine who came through the fierce fighting on Iwo Jima in World War II. Frank was just eighteen, still in Sunday School, when he nearly ran to the recruiting office to enlist in the Marines back in Oklahoma. This was Frank, eager to do all he could for his country. He was a friend of my mother's, a wonderful man my husband and I came to know well. We stayed in touch through the years, and several years ago, Frank moved only a few miles from us here in Farragut, Tennessee to Oak Ridge, Tennessee. It was a joy to see him from time to time.

He passed on only a few months ago, nearly ninety years of age, but I feel he's continuing on in his eternal journey with God. All of us who knew and admired him couldn't help but marvel at his vigor and military posture. He seemed ageless.

Because of my close acquaintance with this former Marine and all the conversations we had about his unique experience and the notes I took, I feel certain he would be pleased that I'm including

an account of this episode in his life in my latest book. He was always keen to talk about Iwo Jima and loaned me some of the books his fellow Marines had written about their experiences. I must admit, some made for grim reading for a woman.

And because of the interest in this particular conflict seems not to have waned much, this first-hand experience will no doubt be something many of my readers throughout the world will enjoy.

Enlisting

Frank enlisted in Oklahoma City, Oklahoma on April 7, 1944. He kept seeing the sign "Uncle Sam wants you!" He wanted to join the Marines because he heard they were sent into combat very soon after training. Frank felt this was the best way to get into battle quickly to defeat the Japanese and help end the war.

Boot Camp

Frank attended Boot Camp in San Diego, California for six weeks. In their discipline training they were told, "Mine is not to ask the reason why, but mine is to obey or die." There was also fitness training, rifle

and bayonet training at Camp Pendleton where Frank was qualified as an expert rifleman. They had island invasion simulation training, as well as gas attack training. Frank was assigned to 5th Marine Division (out of 7 divisions) and "Spearhead" Division after boot camp.

Travel to Training Camp

They traveled to training camp from San Diego, California to Hilo, Hawaii. They traveled on an APA (Attack Transport) 2,511 miles which took about a week and ran into rough weather on the way. From Hilo they went to Kamuela, Hawaii by train on flatcars about 3 to 4 miles away. They went through jungle to a tent camp already in place at Camp Tarawa. There were 3 men to a tent. Kamuela was on a cattle ranch owned by the King Family in Texas. It was a large area with cactus. The Marines found you could eat cactus berries. But if you did, you'd get stickers in your tongues that would last for days. However, the berries were delicious. This is where Frank met Ron Cunningham who rescued Frank from a tent of "Yankees". They became close friends. Played cards, taught each other sports--catch, basketball).

Training and Preparation

In this desert on Hawaii they underwent artillery training. The Marines fired 75mm Pack Howitzer and practiced to prepare and shoot "cannon" or "piece." (Projectile wt. - 15 lbs) They took wire communication training/communication of personnel (CP). They learned to climb a pole and string wires for communication purposes between the artillery weapon and a forward observer.

There was also mental preparation with prayer and study in whatever religious beliefs they held.

Getting ready to go to Iwo Jima

For combat, the Marines went back to Hilo, Hawaii, then on to Pearl Harbor 205 miles away. At Pearl Harbor they could see many ships in preparation for going into combat. They went near Midway Atoll (Island) on the way to Saipan. They went by Saipan -- US Commonwealth of Northern Mariana Islands. They traveled 3,711 miles on the APA. Got off the APA and onto an LST (Landing Ship Tank) to go to Iwo Jima.

Why Iwo Jima Was Chosen for Invasion

I asked Frank this one day, and he said Iwo Jima was
of strategic importance to the US because of its being
only 650 miles south of Tokyo. Also, we needed the
airfields for our distressed bombers to have a place to
land. The island was 3.5 miles long and 1.5 wide at
widest point. (8.5 square miles)
It was shaped like a pork chop and had an extinct
volcano at the southern end called Mount Suribachi.
This was 200 ft. high. (Officially the Mount is 556
ft high, but that measurement is from the ocean
floor.) It is almost the exact height of the Washington
Monument.

American Preparation for Invasion

June 1944, 8 months before the landing on February
19, 945, Iwo Jima was bombed by carriers and land
based planes from the Mariana Islands (near Saipan
and Tinian). The Island was bombed 72 days before
the Marines landed. In all, there were 5800 tons of
bombs with 2700 flights by the 7th Air Force. 70,000
American assault troops got ready for invasion.
There were 485 Navy ships involved in the invasion.
Strafing had no effect! As someone put it, "The
Japanese were not *on* the island, they were *in* it."

Frank's Memories of the Battle on Iwo Jima

They traveled by LST (Landing Ship Tank). The LST was designed to let tanks out on the beach and amphibious vehicles "DUKW" or "ducks" (Detroit United Kirk Words) into the water. The Navy was shooting over their heads, swooshing through the sky. It was exciting. Doors opened on the front on the LST. The DUKW went down a ramp into the water. Frank landed on the 2nd day of battle, February 20, 1945, on a beach at the southeast base of Mount Suribachi.

DUKW Incident - They were driven by Navy men. The wind was high that morning. The waves were huge. Frank's DUKW started to go up the beach. The beach was made of deep, black, volcanic sand. The DUKW could not get enough traction. Wheels were spinning in the sand. The driver backed the DUKW into the water to make another attempt. But the waves were so large from the high wind that DUKW turned parallel to the beach. Then the DUKW turned over in the water and dumped all the Marines out into the water. Frank's friend and fellow Marine, Ronald Cunningham, who had been previously trained to drive a DUKW, knew the driver should never let the vehicle get parallel with the beach because it could turn over, which it did. Before the DUKW turned

over , Ronald got into the front end and said loudly. "Frank, you better jump!" Ronald jumped off safely onto the edge of the beach. Frank stayed down inside of DUKW for protection from being shot at by the Japanese. The next wave turned the DUKW over in the water and dumped those remaining out. While Frank was in the water, a quote from *Science and Health* came to him. "The quote is called the "Scientific Statement of Being" which declares in part: "There is no life, truth intelligence, nor substance in matter. All is infinite Mind and its infinite manifestation…" Frank was not afraid because he had thinking of God's protecting power. When he stood up, the water was up to about his chest. Ronald came down from the beach and reached out his hand to help get Frank out of the way of being hit by the DUKW. The DUKW weighed several thousand pounds, and thus Ronald saved Frank's life that day. Frank was always grateful to Ron for his strong arm and grip to help save his life during the landing. As they were on the beach, a Top Sergeant came up and told them to lay down in the trench until time to go up to the artillery weapons.

Feeling lucky to be alive, Frank later wrote to Top Sergeant Arthur E. Sauter. He was still in the Marine Corps at Camp Lejeune, NC and had attained

the rank of Captain. Frank asked him about his recollection about their landing. He told Frank in his letter, as the DUKW subsided with the wave, it again picked up and appeared to drop on top of Frank. He could have been crushed by at least 2-3 tons of weight. The next 3-4 waves caught the underneath side of the DUKW and turned it every way but loose. The Sergeant had made wise-cracks about all 3 men having to reserve a seat in church to thank God they were still alive.

The DUKW was flooded and finally washed up on the beach with all wheels mashed in toward the undersiding. Later, the entire battalion message center on the shore was lost by one round of 260 mm Jap mortar (9men) and 2 officers (Communications Officer and the Ordinance Officer). After 15 minutes, the Marines crawled up to the weapons. They were located at the south end of the first airfield, near the base of Mt. Suribachi. Frank had a foxhole to rest in right outside of his weapon.

What Frank's Day Was Like

He slept in a fox hole with his uniform on and used his helmet as a pillow. I asked him once, how in the world could anyone sleep with that battle going on?

His reply, you got so sleepy you couldn't help but fall asleep. It didn't matter where you were or what you were doing.

They took turns firing the weapon which was a 75mm Pack Howitzer. Frank would load and fire the weapon. For him to fire the weapon, the 3-striped Sergeant, the man in charge of their artillery weapon with 5 men under him, had communication with the forward observer. They would say, move to left or right to elevate. They could set the timing on the projectile when to explode. If you didn't set it, it would explode on impact. On one occasion, Frank was told to Fire At Will, as fast as he could. Fire, reload, continue. He did for many rounds until the barrel started smoking. The Sergeant said to stop, then mopped the weapon out with water. They were on 4 hours, off 4 hours. Mortar fire dropped in and around the Marines day and night. Each night, there would be a number of flares that the Marines would shoot up into the sky. These flares had parachutes on them and floated down slowly and lit up the whole island. This allowed Marines to see the Japanese more clearly at night.

The Raising of That Flag

Frank observed the flag raising on Mt. Suribachi on February 23, 1945, on Frank's 4th day on Iwo Jima. A sight never to be forgotten, a sight that when I see it in documentaries on WWII feel such a thrill. And I wasn't there nearby. Frank said when this happened, e*veryone* was yelling, "Look at the flag!" Frank turned back and saw the flag from where he was, about 300 yards away. He could see it clearly. This was a tremendous morale booster. The ships offshore were also sounding their horns in celebration. They could tell they were winning the battle.

Pancakes on a Shovel

I asked Frank about their food and he said now and then they would have a power bar which tasted so good. Much like one of our granola bars I imagine. The Marine sergeant knew his Marines had been eating C-rations and K-rations. In order to give them something more pleasant to eat, he thought of cooking some pancakes on a shovel. The CB's (Construction Battalion) a.k.a. "Sea-Bees" were professional road builders and able to build things that were needed. They had access to good food. So the Sergeant went to the CB's and got ingredients

for pancakes. They didn't have syrup, so the Marines contributed marmalade from their rations. In the rations, they had tropical butter that wouldn't melt in the sun. So they had tropical butter with marmalade on pancakes. And Frank said they tasted SO good.

Fighting Over

Fighting had stopped. They *thought* it was over. But Frank and his Sergeant were on one side of the sand bag emplacement and Frank on the other, when without warning a bullet came through the opening of the north end of the emplacement and hit a sand bag between them and exploded. The emplacement was a round place with sand bags all around, with camouflage cover on the top, and with an opening towards the north where the artillery pointed out. When the sand bag exploded, a fragment from the shell nicked the sergeant just below his left eyes. The Sergeant immediately went to a first-aid station and had it taken care of. The Sergeant eventually received a purple heart for that wound.

Another Glorious Sight

When the battle for Iwo Jima finished about 2-3 days later, the Marines could hear airplanes coming. They turned out to be the "Blue Angels Air Force." They

flew over the middle part of northern Iwo Jima, then flew straight up in the air, twisted clockwise, rising to a great height (about 1 mile) with white smoke coming out of the back of each plane. There were 5 airplanes in that group, which flew in close formation, then left the island to return to their aircraft carrier. This flight exhibit was to show American victory in the battle for Iwo Jima. The flight was beautiful, Frank told me, spectacular and a joy to behold! A great celebration to witness! All on the island and nearby ships could observe the show.

At Last, a Shower

Frank's last day on Iwo Jima was day 26. Total combat was 36 days and Frank's was 24 days. He told he was about 20 lbs. thinner when it was over. When the fighting stopped on that side of the island, the Marines boarded a ship. When they got aboard the ship, they were loading a number of wounded Marines. It was a pathetic sight. They were severely injured. The Marines were allowed to take a shower for the first time since they landed. They were allowed about 5 minutes in the shower because fresh water aboard the ship was limited. Frank told me, "You cannot imagine how good that shower felt!" "Yes, I can", I told him.

Frank said in his book, "Marine Veteran Frank L. Pryor - WWII Remembrances" (2009):

"I attribute the wonderful way in which I was protected in combat to my study of and diligent devotion to the teachings of Christian Science and the prayerful work of relatives and friends."

And finally on the subject of his religious beliefs which he held all his life, Frank told me he took with him into basic training, the intensified training in Hawaii, and on the ship and into battle what is called the service editions of the Bible and *Science and Health*. They were very small and could be carried by the servicemen. The Christian Science Church in Boston furnished these special editions to servicemen. I myself have a copy of each which I keep in my car.

Even during those three weeks on the island of Iwo Jima when things were quieter, Frank told me he would read the daily Bible Lesson from his two books. Remarkable what these men went through, and how they were able to have some semblance of normality nonetheless.

Australian Soldier:
Close Calls in the Jungle

Paul, a very close friend of ours from Melbourne, Australia shared with us some of his harrowing experiences when he saw service in WWII in the Solomon Islands.

At one point, he was in a foxhole and what he said had to be God's leading, felt he must get out of that place at once. There was no immediate reason for doing this, but he obeyed divine direction. The very instant he was out, a Japanese shell exploded right where he would have been sitting.

Another time they were going across a raging stream in the jungle on a rope. The rope slipped down, and it looked as though he would drown for sure. But he was pulled to safety just in time. "It was a close run thing", he said. Paul told us what saved him was something he tried to keep always in thought when he was fighting there in the jungle, something that had made an impression on him from his days in the Christian Science Sunday School. The teacher told them in one session that they were one with God, that God was with them in every circumstance

they faced, no matter what they were doing or where they might be. God would take care of them, as they were His own loved child.

Paul at the end of his deployment contracted malaria. He was sent back home to convalesce. He told us it looked as though he might not make it through. A man who had served as a Chaplain in the Pacific theater of war was enlisted to pray for him, to give him Christian Science treatment. Paul was finally completely healed of this challenging condition, and was ever after so grateful to our heavenly Father for His help.

When Animals Need Help

It was a scary night for us. One of our dogs was apparently bitten by a spider or some poisonous insect one evening. Dylan was on the back porch, and although screened-in did have floorboards with some space between them. We knew immediately something was wrong when he stood up shakily to get to the door. He could hardly walk and was quite ill it was clear. We managed to get him up on a bed, even though he's a large 70-lb dog. We love the vet we have, but he wouldn't have been available at that hour of the night. And we didn't want to take our beloved dog to an emergency place we weren't familiar with.

Being accustomed to turning to God when trouble arises, my husband and I both reached out for divine aid. I sat down on the rug next to the bed and prayed for all I was worth. John went to his office so he could turn away from the suffering, while he prayed. For me, the human picture was daunting and my fear was nearly overwhelming at first. But soon I felt divine Love's presence surrounding us all. And after a couple of hours, Dylan became quieter, then fell asleep.

As I shared with a friend later, I felt certain that had we gotten our dog into the car and driven to the emergency hospital, not to mention probably having to wait to see a vet, then have tests done, Dylan might not have made it through that night. It was the immediacy of God's help that we were so thankful for.

To our immense relief the next morning, he could get down from the bed under his own steam. We took him out for short walk in our woods. Oh the joy we felt to see him recover so quickly and completely.

If I had never experienced any other proof of what God's power can do in one's life than this, it would be enough for me.

As it happens with most pet owners, I suppose, there have been other episodes where God's help was needed. Dear, sweet, innocent creatures are so often receptive to such help we have found, and we thank God it's always at hand to turn to.

Another time I was just leaving our driveway very early in the morning when a dog appeared that I didn't know. He obviously didn't feel at all well, and was staggering a bit. Then of all things, he collapsed

right by my car. My husband was out of town, and I didn't want to go knock on a neighbor's door at that hour. This was a very large dog, and I didn't think I could get him into my car to take him to a vet somewhere, had I found one open. What to do?

Almost at once, I started praying. This statement from *Science and Health* came to thought and I worked mentally from that standpoint. It reads: "Mind is the source of all movement, and there is no inertia to retard or check its perpetual and harmonious action."

Quite soon, the dog got up and trotted off as if nothing had happened. This was so good to see, how quickly God helped that dear animal. Later on one of our walks through the back streets with our dog, I saw this animal in what must have been his yard and he looked just fine.

If Only

If only I had been stronger in my Christian beliefs back then, my life would have had far fewer challenges. Perhaps for many of us this is true.

I recall one incident in my college days when Jesus' teachings were just beginning to speak to me. A misunderstanding erupted with a relative and I wanted to apologize to her, say I was wrong, make peace with her. But another aunt said, "Oh don't do that! She'll think you're weak." So I let the moment pass and didn't discover until years later the strength that comes to us when we practice the humility and love Christ enjoined upon us. I regret this.

Anyone who thinks doing what Jesus asks of us is easy just is not doing it, is all I can say. It calls for nothing short of the most manly manliness one can imagine who hasn't tried it.

Another sharp reminder of how much less anguish there would have been had the circumstances been handled differently: there I was just sitting in my downtown Boston office one fine day when the phone rang. It was the Editor of magazines I had

been writing for. He was previously in advertising in Australia, had a different writing style from mine, and decided one day he didn't want to publish me anymore. There were a couple of manuscripts in the department awaiting publication and he said, "I don't intend to publish these!" I was devastated. It felt like someone had slammed me against a wall. Panicky, I thought, "What other outlet will I have now for my writing? I'll just die if I can't write." He seemed to me like the meanest man that ever walked down a city street.

I stopped writing for awhile. This was one miserable time. But eventually I did start up again, and by this time, that Editor had moved on and the new man actually thought my essays had something to say to the world.

When I recovered my composure that challenging afternoon of the phone call, I called a close friend to see if he had time to talk with me. His office was nearby, so I made an appointment. As I sat across from his desk, pouring out my distress, my "I don't know what to do. Whom should take this problem to?" this wise and experienced man said after a time, "Why not take it to God?" His words went right over my head. I just wasn't spiritually seasoned

enough to rely on God at this point, to even begin doing things His way. I still thought, there is some higher-up who may help me through this. Higher up human, that is.

Though a few years down the road of life unfolded before I could appreciate what my friend was driving at that day, it did finally dawn on me the wisdom of doing just that. As I have experienced the superior help that accompanies our doing this when life gets tough, it seems to me in looking back that an angel had recommended this. To this day, I'm grateful for what my friend said that day. And that I now see how far better it is to take our problems to God first. Then, whatever individuals are needed to assist in solutions, our loving Father will see that we have them. In any case, we'll always be lifted out of feelings of fear and helplessness when life deals us its unexpected blows.

The Radical Difference Christ Makes

Am I suggesting that once we make Christ the focus of our life and look to God for all that makes life worth living, all challenges will suddenly cease. In no way. There will be sharp struggles. But our day-to-day experience becomes through Christ much more alive -- happier, healthier, freer. Life becomes for us a real adventure. And in the situations that once would have defeated us, we now find ourselves having the mastery.

Satan's attacks on us take different forms. One of the worst I've had to overcome is discouragement. It has seemed to drop on me like a block of concrete. "Give up, it isn't worth it" can nearly overwhelm at times.

Awhile back a devoted Christian said to me, "Discouragement has had me down for the count, not sure I could get up and continue the fight." The carnal mind's attempts to shut down our work for Christ can leave many of us saying amen to this.

But you know what? God came to the aid of my friend, as He always does for you and me. And

speaking personally, I have been brought out of opposition so intense it seemed I could not endure it another minute. And what caused this? The blessed plain-speaking of our Master. Jesus never promised His followers a picnic on sunny days with balmy breezes. We have only to consider words like these to know better:

"Blessed are ye when men shall revile you, and persecute you,
And shall say all manner of evil against you falsely, for my sake."

"If the world hate you, ye know that it hated me before it hated you."

"If ye were of the world, the world would love his own; but because
ye are not of the world, but I have chosen you out of the
world, therefore the world hateth you."

"Remember the word that I said unto you, The servant is not
greater than his lord. If they have persecuted me, they will
also persecute you."

So comforting, so bracing I always find. And there is this which always lifts me up when I think about it. Those of us following in Jesus footsteps have the joy of knowing that we're in holy company indeed. To think about all those men and women through the ages who have given their all to be true to Christ never fails to renew my resolve to press on.

Our Saviour met every attack of the carnal mind and came through to victory. And he said to his followers then, and to all in all time to come:

"Behold, I give unto you power to tread on serpents and scorpions, and over all the power of the enemy: and nothing shall by any means hurt you."

Another thing that always works for me when hard-pressed is giving thanks to God. Before I get through reviewing all the things He has brought me through, all the daily blessings He pours out on us, the darkness lifts and I begin feeling more like my usual happy self.

I have a friend in Florida who is such an inspiration to me, and to all who know her. Betty is the most thankful person I've ever known. And it isn't because she has always had smooth sailing in her

life. Far from it. With an ill relative who required an enormous amount of time from her a few years ago, with financial challenges that seemed daunting at times, this small, one would almost say, delicate little lady, kept sweet through it all. Each day she would pray, "Dear God, let the words of my mouth, and the meditations of my heart, be acceptable in thy sight, O Lord, my strength and my redeemer." And she would add to what the Psalmist wrote, "And the expression on my face and the tone of my voice, too." Being a committed follower of Christ Jesus, she intended to live as Christlike a life as she could, and knew that even the looks she gave to people and the tone of her voice needed to express not impatience and irritation, but patience and kindness. It wasn't always easy, but she worked at it. I wouldn't have wanted to, and indeed could not have, walked in this lady's shoes for a week.

More than once, Betty would say to me, "Just think, we're heirs of God and joint-heirs with Christ!" Betty is an ardent student of the Bible and of the teachings of Christian Science, and I feel sure this is what has sustained her.

No Walk in the Park

Walking the path Jesus trod is not, cannot be, this. But we can take heart. Those of us who have named the name of Christ will always have the victory over evil. *Always.*

I've come to the realization of two things about this: if I go down into the valley of defeatism, I'll just have to lift myself up again. And, it isn't us the devil is primarily after but that our service to God may be interfered with, if not outright stopped for good.

I've often marveled at those early Christians who chose to undergo unspeakable tortures rather than renounce Christ. I have asked myself, could I stand up under what they went through? But as I've matured in my spiritual journey, and survived onslaughts of the devil myself, it has become clear that there is nothing else one could do. Turning our backs on Him is unthinkable, so we resolve to go on, no matter what is dealt out to us. And there is this: we can take comfort in knowing how many thousands before us, and individuals now, are standing up for their beliefs under incredible hardships.

The woman who founded my religion, Mary Baker Eddy, once wrote something that has always inspired me. "Admiral Coligny, in the time of the French Huguenots, was converted to Protestantism through a stray copy of the Scriptures that fell into his hands. He replied to his wife, who urged him to come out and confess his faith. "It is wise to count the cost of becoming a true Christian.' She answered him, 'It is wiser to count the cost of *not* becoming a true Christian.' So, whatever we meet that is hard in the Christian warfare we must count as nothing, and must think instead, of our poverty and helplessness without this understanding, and count ourselves always as debtors to Christ, Truth." *Miscellaneous Writings*

And in the words of our blessed Master: "In the world ye shall have tribulation; but be of good cheer; I have overcome the world."

Heroes of the Faith

This is what I call those men and women throughout history who have stood up for what they believed, who refused to strike their colors under often extreme conditions, and under threat of death in some cases. In so doing, they have left the most uplifting examples for the rest of us.

Something I loved doing when we lived in Massachusetts and I worked in downtown Boston was visiting the Boston Public Library. Their reading room is something to see, and as I understand, this library is one of the world's best. It still is to me. The sacred hours I spent there! I would ride home on the commuter train back to the suburbs feeling I was on holy ground.

Anyway, what sparked my reading and research was wanting to know more about certain leading lights of the Christian faith. Luminaries for sure. I was eager to know about their lives, to read what they wrote down about their experiences. Some of the writings were in the rare book section, and what a privilege to be allowed access to these. The wealth of inspiration I gained! I even began keeping a notebook

on my visits, and have several filled with glowing words of wisdom and encouragement for others who have named the Name of Christ and are endeavoring to follow in His steps.

My Hero of all Heroes, for all time to come, is Jesus Himself. This goes without saying.

Following are individuals who have had a tremendous and long-lasting influence for good on my life. I could, of course, list so many more.

Martin Luther

A giant among Christian writers and doers. Rightly regarded as the founder of the sixteenth-century Protestant Reformation -- the religious, political, cultural and social revolution that broke the hold of the Catholic Church over Europe.

Martin Luther's vast writings have thrilled me over and over, and have caused me to feel that had I been there in his day, I may well have joined up in his fight for religious freedom. Spiritually on fire is one way to describe them.

I could quote endlessly from things Luther said, but this one I especially treasure:

"I cannot choose but to adhere to the word of God, which has possession of my conscience; nor can I possibly, nor will I even make any recantation, since it is neither safe nor honest to act contrary to conscience! Here I stand; I cannot do otherwise, so help me God! Amen."

To think of the countless men and women down the years who have taken renewed courage from just these few words. I know I have.

Martin Luther is most widely known for criticizing aspects of the Roman Catholic Church. In particular he believed that it was the Bible and not the Catholic Church which was the source of legitimacy for interpreting the word of Christ. He also translated the Bible into German, making it more accessible to the general public.

Luther became a student at the University of Efurt in 1501. He studied Aristotle and was drawn to philosophy and theology. However, he was unsatisfied. Therefore, he decided to become a monk and devote his life to God. But as a monk, he felt a spiritual dryness.

In 1517, Luther first protested to the Catholic Church about the sale of indulgences (the full or partial remission of temporal punishment due for sins which have already been forgiven.) He argued that it was faith alone that could provide for the remission of sin and not monetary payments.

The church was slow to respond to the criticisms Luther made, and in this period he became a prolific writer. His writings were widely distributed throughout Europe.

On October 31, 1517, Luther posted 95 theses condemning practices of the church on the door of the Castle Church of Wittenberg. He also posted a handwritten copy to the archbishop of Magdeburg, Albert of Mainz. The 95 theses were critical of many things relating to baptism and the sale of indulgences for the remittance of sin. He also indirectly challenged the Pope's legitimacy:

"Why does the pope, whose wealth today is greater than the wealth of the richest Crassus, build the basilica of Saint Peter with the money of poor believers rather than with his own money?" he asked.

Within a few weeks, Luther's theses had spread throughout Germany. The significance of this written challenge caused the church to respond. On June 15, 1520, Pope Leo X issued a formal rebuttal to Luther's Ninety-Five Theses, a papal encyclical titled "Exsurge Domine -- "Arise, O Lord".

However, by this time, Luther's criticisms were widely in circulation; and with the help of the new printing presses, the reformation movement gained strength and popularity. The Catholic Church would never have the same unchallenged authority in Europe again.

Luther was ex-communicated in 1520 for refusing to recant. In April 1521, the enforcement of banning his writings fell to the secular authorities. Luther acknowledged that he was the author of the writings but again refused to recant them. Saying he would stand by them, Luther was condemned as an outlaw and thereafter he feared for his life.

He wrote substantially at one point, "If you want to change the world, pick up your pen and write." Martin Luther certainly did this and succeeded in changing his and our world beyond all expectation.

William Tyndale

I can scarcely read about this man's stupendous achievement without having to put the book down at times, almost in tears. He brought out the first printed New Testament in English -- a sacred text and controversial publication, in 1526. He later translated the complete Bible. His work was pronounced heretical in England, so his Bibles were smuggled into the country in bales of cloth. Those discovered owning them were punished. At first only the books were destroyed, but soon heretics would be burned too--including Tyndale himself in 1536.

Prior to this, a priest one day openly attacked his beliefs. He replied, "If God spare my life, before very long I shall cause a plough boy to know the scriptures better than you do!"

The British Library calls his Bible "the most important printed book in the English language." Think of this! They bought a copy in 1994 for a little over a million pounds.

Tyndale was imprisoned for 18 months under the most wretched conditions and for what crime?

Making the Word of God available to the common man. So often on a cold winter's night when I've crawled into a warm, safe bed, I think of something he wrote to a friend during this time, that he suffered terribly from sleeping on the cold stone floor with only a thin garment on. He asked if he could be brought something warm to wear.

How can we lovers of the Bible ever be grateful enough for what this one divinely-inspired, God-upheld man wrought!

William Tyndale's mighty work forms a significant part of modern Bible translations.

"I had perceived by experience, how that it was impossible to stablish the lay people in any truth, except the scripture were plainly laid before their eyes in their mother tongue, that they might see the process, order, and meaning of the text", he once wrote.

To start with his earlier life, Tyndale began studying theology at Oxford University in 1516. But, he was highly critical of the idea that one had to study so long before actually being allowed to study the Bible.

Influenced by ideas of the Reformation, he became increasingly known as a man of unorthodox and radical religious views. In particular, he was keen to translate the New Testament into English. He believed this would help ordinary people understand scripture directly and not through the filter of the church. In this, Tyndale was influenced by ideas of Martin Luther. Tyndale would claim that the Bible does not support the Roman Catholic Church's view that they were the body of Christ on earth.

After leaving Cambridge, Tyndale was criticised by some around him for his radical viewpoints. In 1523, he left for London hoping to translate the Bible into English. However, he struggled to receive any support or backing and so left for the continent.

When I read this, it called to thought something Albert Schweitzer once wrote, "If anyone proposes to do some good in this world, he must not expect people to roll stones out of his path. He must not be surprised if they roll a few more upon it."

How often this is the experience of reformers and doers of great deeds. If only things had been easier, I often think. Why did it have to be so uphill for most of them?

During his time on the continent, he visited Luther and wrote extensively on scriptures and continued his translations of the Bible.

"I never altered one syllable of God's Word against my conscience" he wrote, "nor would do this day, if all that is in earth, whether it be honor, pleasure, or riches, might be given me."

Cardinal Wolsey denounced Tyndale as a heretic in 1529. In 1530, he wrote a treatise critical of Henry VIII's divorce. When the English King found out he was furious and sought Tyndale's extradition.

After being in hiding for several years, in 1535 Tyndale was betrayed and handed over to the imperial authorities in Belgium. There he languished in prison for many months, and was finally hanged and burned. His last words were reported to be: "Lord! Open the King of England's eyes."

John Bunyan

He was an eighteenth century English writer and preacher, author of the religious allegory, "The Pilgrim's Progress". What interested me in this man, apart from reading his tremendous book, was learning about the twelve years he spent in gaol. He refused to give up preaching God's Word, and chose rather to take the punishment meted out to him.

And when I read his description of the great anxiety he underwent as he sat there in jail, worrying how his family was going to survive without him there, how they would even have enough to eat, I found myself very moved. How well any of us who love our family can appreciate the agony this caused.

Following is one of the verses from his famous book. It captivated me years ago, and has been one of my favorites through the years:

(From "The Pilgrim's Progress" by John Bunyan)

O world of wonders! (I can say no less)

That I should be preserved in that distress

That I have met with here! O blessed be

That hand that from it hath delivered me!

Dangers in darkness, devils, Hell, and sin,

Did compass me, while I this Vale was in;

Yes, snares, and pits, and traps, and nets did lie

My path about, that worthless silly I

Might have been catched, entangled, and cast down;

But since I live let JESUS wear the Crown.

John Bunyan was the most famous of the Puritan writers and preachers. He was born in Elstow, England in 1628. He is most well-known today for his book, "The Pilgrim's Progress", one of the most printed books in history, which he composed while in prison for the crime of preaching the Gospel without a license.

He was no scholar, except of the English Bible, but that he knew thoroughly. He also drew much influence from Martin Luther's "Commentary on the Epistle to the Galatians."

John Wesley

He was an eighteenth century English evangelist and founder of the Wesleyan Tradition. He is considered the father of Methodism.

It was a joy to be sitting there in the Boston Public Library, getting to know this remarkable follower of Christ. It was always so uplifting, almost holy at times.

Of all the things I know about this saintly little man, one of the experiences he went through stands out. He was preaching outdoors one day since the Anglican Church doors were closed to him, and some rowdies stirred up the crowd milling around him. One individual hurled a brick, which caught Wesley on the side of the head. He fell to the ground. But this is what amazed me when I read it. He was helped up, and according to several eye-witnesses, maintained his Christly composure. Wesley was not resentful, didn't try to retaliate against these individuals, but forgave them, staying loving and sweet through the whole ordeal. In his words, "I very nearly slept with my fathers under the altar." It obviously could have ended his career right then, but of course God had further work for him to do. And so many people are

the blessed beneficiaries that there was.

John Wesley is known for two things: co-founding Methodism and his tremendous work ethic. In the 1700's, when land travel was by walking, horseback, or carriage, Wesley logged more than 4,000 miles a year. During his lifetime he preached about 40,000 sermons.

Wesley could give today's experts lessons in efficiency. He was a natural organizer and approached everything diligently, especially religion. It was at Oxford University in England that he and his brother Charles participated in a Christian club in such an orderly manner that critics called them methodists. It was a title which they gladly embraced.

As priests in the Church of England, John and Charles traveled from Great Britain to Georgia, in the American colonies, in 1735. He was appointed pastor of the church in Savannah.

When he imposed church discipline on members who failed to notify him that they were taking communion, Wesley found himself accused in civil courts by one of the powerful families of Savannah. The jury was stacked against him.

John Wesley returned to England bitter, disillusioned and spiritually low. On May 24, 1738 a friend convinced him to go to a meeting. Here is Wesley's description of that momentous event:

"In the evening I went very unwillingly to a society in Aldersgate Street, where one was reading Luther's preface to the "Epistle to the Romans." About a quarter before nine, while he was describing the change which God works in the heart through faith in Christ, I felt my heart strangely warmed. I felt I did trust in Christ, Christ alone for salvation, and an assurance was given me that he had taken away my sins, even mine, and saved me from the law of sin and death."

This "Aldersgate Experience" had a permanent effect on Wesley's life. He answered a request from fellow preacher George Whitefield to join him in Whitefield's evangelism ministry. Whitefield preached outdoors, something unheard of at the time.

As always, Wesley went about his new work methodically. He organized groups into societies, than classes, connections, and circuits, under the direction of a supervisor. He saw great opportunity outside England and ordained two lay preachers

to serve in the newly independent United States of America. Methodism was breaking away from the Church of England as a separate Christian denomination.

Meanwhile, John Wesley continued to preach throughout the British Isles. Never one to waste time, he discovered that he could read while walking, on horseback, or in carriage. Nothing stopped him. Wesley pushed on during rainstorms and blizzards, and if his coach got stuck, he continued on horseback or on foot.

Robert E. Lee

My interest in this man of marble-like character stems not from a fascination with the American Civil War nor from being a daughter of the South where General Lee is still revered by many. It is due to the way he came through the conflict. While a great honor to be called to a meeting with an associate of Abraham Lincoln and asked to lead the Union Army, Lee declined the offer, choosing to not fight against Virginia which was his home. As he led the Army of Northern Virginia in the war, the weight of responsibility on this man's shoulders must have been immense. And toward the end of those years, to know his Confederate soldiers were hungry, and walking along those dusty roads in tattered shoes, if not barefoot, must have been nearly unbearable for him.

I have read everything out there on this man, and what has stood out to me, and inspired me so, was his faith in God. He said the only way he could have endured all he went through was this living faith.

And many of his troops would hear him pray these words, which he prayed nearly every single day:

"Have I thanked you enough today, dear Father, for Your unspeakable gift?"

Just think of the ennobling influence on those soldiers who heard him pray this. And all those thousands of people through the years who have read these words.

At the age of 46, Lee experienced a spiritual awakening and was confirmed at Christ Church.

Lee is no doubt one of the most respected figures on the stage of human history. The love, admiration and respect given to the man is universal, revered by his peers, respected by his enemies.

As one learns about Lee, he discovers that the rock on which he built his life, the river that ran deep through his soul that gave him strength and sustained him, that led him to attain to such heights and carry on in the face of bitter defeat, was a total devotion to and humble serving of his Lord and Saviour, Jesus Christ. The teachings of Christ and the words of the Holy Scriptures shone forth in the walk and life of Robert E. Lee. In addition, his own writings demonstrate his profound faith.

He prayed for his enemies and when he was President of Washington College in Lexington, Virginia, Lee showed he had a heart for all non-believers. He remarked to a friend who was a preacher as they walked near the College one day:

"I shall be disappointed, sir, I shall fail in the leading object that brought me here, unless the young men all become real Christians; and I wish you and others of your sacred profession to do all you can to accomplish this result."

Mary Baker Eddy

From early childhood, this remarkable woman was a close and devoted student of the Bible. She was an influential American author, teacher, and religious leader, noted for her groundbreaking ideas about spirituality and health, which she named Christian Science. She articulated those ideas in her major work, *Science and Health with Key to the Scriptures.* Four years later she founded the Church of Christ, Scientist which today has branch churches and societies around the world.

I wouldn't have the life I now have without the influence of this woman, and will be forever thankful she was brought through all she had to endure in her early years. "I love Jesus more than any man who ever was or is" she once wrote. And what drove her on through tribulation was an overwhelming desire to bring to mankind the laws of God that were the basis of Jesus' healing work, and that had lifted her out of death.

At one point, she was to give a talk in a New England town and some people threatened to blow up the hall. What did this nineteenth century, refined

lady do? She didn't seek human protection. In her own words, "I leaned on God, and was safe."

Of all the inspired words this woman has left, I think this the most sublime. It sums up, to me, what sustained her in giving the world her discovery. "I can endure anything, if I just don't incur His displeasure."

What more can I say about a woman who certainly ranks among heroic Christians in my estimation? The healings recounted in this book, the freedom I've gained from physical afflictions certainly (and this is no small thing) gives some idea of how highly I regard her.

I was driving along the other day and happened to recall something I'd read about her early days in Massachusetts when she was working on her book. She would take a break from the writing, and walk down to the rocky shore of the Atlantic Ocean to a famous landmark, Red Rock, climb up on it, and sit there for awhile. How could anyone have foreseen what God had in store for His servant. Looking out over that ocean, she would have been amazed had someone told her then that years later, in the vast Pacific Ocean, a young Marine would recall some words from this book as he was almost drowning in

the water there, and find God's protecting power.

This, and thousands of other experiences that were to come in the lives of those who embraced her discovery, would have been enough to repay her for the years of poverty, friendlessness, opposition, extreme loneliness, even hunger at times, as she pushed on to do what she was sure God was calling her to do.

Coming Through Storms

A workable knowledge of God is urgently needed when we face a storm of some kind.

Speaking of God, the Bible states: "For thou hast been a strength to the poor, a strength to the needy in his distress, a refuge from the storm, a shadow from the heat, when the blast of the terrible ones is as a storm against the wall."

Christian Science has shown me how to make these words practical, how to turn to God with the assurance of experiencing proof of His strength.

What makes it possible to stand up against the buffeting winds of life's problems? Reverent, regular communion with God, man's divine, unfailingly loving source.

In general, people see to it that their houses, possessions, and lives are adequately insured. How much more important to have our lives protected spiritually!

When we have something to overcome (and

who that is journeying heavenward hasn't?), we ought to rejoice rather than complain--rejoice that we have the wherewithal for the overcoming. At times, the faithful face difficult challenges. But they also have much with which to meet them. Jesus' assurances are ever at hand to uplift you and me, to bring us through any tumult to peace. And inharmony does pass--always. Being unreal, without divine support or recognition, the devil's days are inevitably numbered. Spiritual awakening always comes to those who hold to the facts of existence and refuse to be swept from the straight path of trust in God's ever presence and all-power.

Courage is an indispensable element of standing up to mortal claims of power--that moral courage Jesus expressed when he healed in defiance of material so-called laws. Everyone has courage, but it must be cultivated, exercised. At the start, one may only be able to feel resolved to face up to a fear or danger. Next comes that first step of spiritual rebellion, along with strength from having taken it. Then other steps of joy, gratitude, persistence, follow until reality is actually glimpsed and the needed freedom comes about.

Being able to stand through stormy times is essential for the follower of Christ, which is not a way of life for the fainthearted or shallow of purpose. Having our understanding put to the test sometimes startles us, when sober reflection on the life of our Master would leave no doubt as the withstanding and winning in store for us.

The carnal mind's opposition to one's spiritual progress can take many forms. When one is in the very midst of a stormy time, he may have little certainty of reaching his destination, not so much a glimpsing a road sign to tell him how far he yet to go.

What does one do? The only thing he can do: walk on, keep on trusting God's strengthening, upholding power to bring him securely through. Challenges, if courageously withstood and overcome through faith in God, are a giant step forward.

As I have learned from the teachings of my religion, effectual communion with God necessarily includes the recognition that man is not a buffeted-about mortal who has to struggle to be free. He is already free in God's sight. He is already at peace. Man is at one with God, divine Mind, who maintains His divine idea precisely in the way He made him-

-complete, perfect. In the reality of our being, dominion is already ours in unlimited degree, because what God is, man reflects. For the human being to prove this may demand some mighty wrestlings. But one can rejoice that he *can* progressively prove himself beyond the reach of severe challenges, eternally safe in God's sheltering arms.

One who professes Jesus as his Exemplar cannot honestly consider that he is following in his steps--or even making any progress down that path--if he runs away during the storms of life. At work in the righteous cause of Christianity, we need never shrink from having our spiritual mettle tested.

Joy Forever Lasting

The blessings God does give to those who stand with Him!

As I was driving along recently, I had on Felix Mendelssohn's oratorio, "Elijah". What a sublime thing it is, too. I couldn't help thinking about his experience of coming across a New Testament one day and reading something Jesus said. His conversion to Christianity was immediate and lasting. But the part of this piece of music that stood out to me was this: "Then shall the righteous shine forth as the sun in their heavenly Father's realm. *Joy on their heads shall be forever lasting.*

To think what those Christian heroes of history are enjoying now. And what awaits you and me as we become, and are now, righteous which means to me being right with God as much as we can, living our lives as His Son made plain for us. This, as I am finding, brings into our lives here and now that joy that will never wane.